BOTS

TINNY'S TINY SECRET

by Russ Bolts
illustrated by Jay Cooper

LITTLE SIMON

New York London Toronto Sydney New Delhi

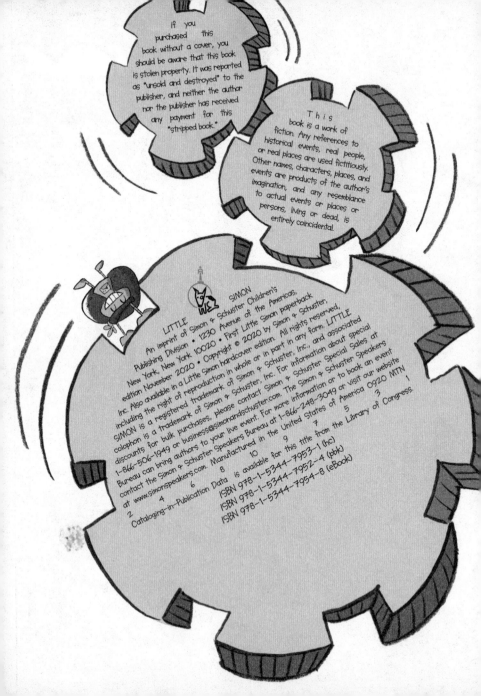

LITTLE SIMON
An imprint of Simon & Schuster Children's Publishing Division • 1230 Avenue of the Americas, New York, New York 10020 • Copyright © 2020 by Simon & Schuster, Inc. Also available in a Little Simon hardcover edition. All rights reserved, including the right of reproduction in whole or in part in any form. LITTLE SIMON is a registered trademark of Simon & Schuster, Inc., and associated colophon is a trademark of Simon & Schuster, Inc. For information about special discounts for bulk purchases, please contact Simon & Schuster Special Sales at 1-866-506-1949 or business@simonandschuster.com. The Simon & Schuster Speakers Bureau can bring authors to your live event. For more information or to book an event contact the Simon & Schuster Speakers Bureau at 1-866-248-3049 or visit our website at www.simonspeakers.com. Manufactured in the United States of America 0920 MTN

First Little Simon paperback edition November 2020

2   4   6   8   10   9   7   5   3   1

Cataloging-in-Publication Data is available for this title from the Library of Congress.

ISBN 978-1-5344-7953-1 (hc)
ISBN 978-1-5344-7952-4 (pbk)
ISBN 978-1-5344-7954-8 (eBook)

CONTENTS

A-ha! I think you don't know and you're trying to act like you know. And if I tell the fans what the Big Blooper is, then I'll also be telling you!
Just tell everyone what it is.
You know the gross gunky stuff you find in weird Bot places? Like the gunk behind your antenna.
The sludge between your treads.

9

Unfortunately, not everyone loved school that day.

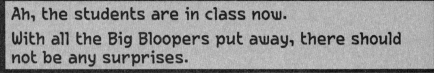

Ah, the students are in class now.
With all the Big Bloopers put away, there should not be any surprises.

Certainly some good kids are sent to the Principal's office for awards or prizes for being so good.

45

51

CHAPTER 5
Tinny Trouble

Meanwhile, back in class, Tinny was very happy.

A Tiny Secret

And so Tinny took off through the halls in search of Joe and Rob.

SCHOOL
PLAY
SIGN-UP

69

75

83

GRAB!

OIL

BEND!

TAPE!

Wow, these dummies look just like the real dummies.

FREEDOM!

95

101

104

115

Trophy Time

In case you were worried about the school, don't. Tinny's plan worked, and all the students were very excited.

119